A LITTLE SPOT OF OPTIMISM

To my children, Ryan and Anna

All inquiries about this book can be sent to the author at
info@dianealber.com
Published in the United States by Diane Alber Art LLC
For more information, or to book an event, visit our website:
www.dianealber.com
ISBN 978-1-951287-29-0
Paperback
Printed in China

This OPTIMISM book belongs to:

_____

_____

_____

Hi, I'm a little SPOT of OPTIMISM!

I'm here to help you learn how to "Look on the bright side." That phrase is called a figure of speech. It means when you are faced with a disappointing situation, you can focus on the POSITIVE, instead of the NEGATIVE.

When you are able
to refocus your THOUGHTS,
it is also called,
shifting your MINDSET!

Your MINDSET determines how you handle a situation.

When you are able to shift your MINDSET with POSITIVE WORDS and ACTIONS it can become easier to PERSEVERE in challenging situations.

If you choose NEGATIVE WORDS, then your NEGATIVE THOUGHTS get TOO BIG. When that happens, it can make you very SAD and can even make you feel sick.

I'm going to show you some WORDS that you can use to shift your THOUGHTS from NEGATIVE to POSITIVE.

Let's look at the time when you lost your soccer game. You were very SAD and disappointed. Instead of letting your SELF-TALK focus on the NEGATIVE...

To shift a **NEGATIVE THOUGHT** to a **POSITIVE THOUGHT**, you need to be aware of how you talk to yourself.

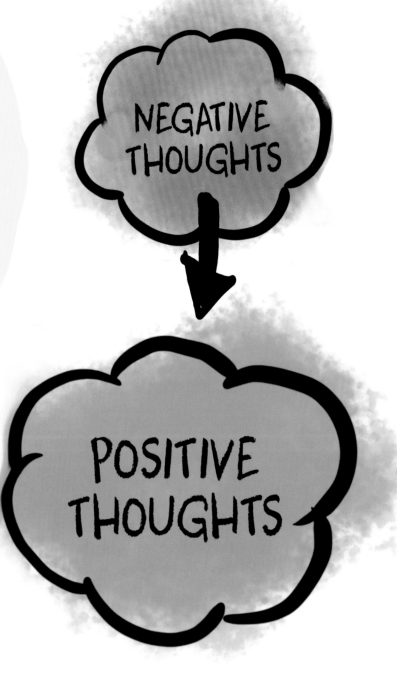

NEGATIVE THOUGHTS → POSITIVE THOUGHTS

I can't do this! → I have to practice.

I made a mistake. → Mistakes help me learn.

This is too hard. → It's just going to take some time and effort to to figure out.

Look how these small changes made all the difference! Another trick is to ask yourself these questions: What good can come from this? What can I learn from this? Is there someone who can help me?

After something good happens, give yourself credit! Think about how you made that outcome successful. Think about all your strengths that helped you succeed!

I'm glad I had the PERSEVERANCE to keep trying to make the tower stable.

Look at failure as an OPPORTUNITY.
When something doesn't go as planned,
always ask yourself, "What can I do
differently next time? Why did that happen?"

This is a great OPPORTUNITY to
learn a new way to do something.